PRINCESS PULVERIZER

Bad moooove!

PENGUIN WORKSHOP
Penguin Young Readers Group
An Imprint of Penguin Random House LLC

Penguin supports copyright. Copyright fuels creativity, encourages diverse
voices, promotes free speech, and creates a vibrant culture. Thank you
for buying an authorized edition of this book and for complying with
copyright laws by not reproducing, scanning, or distributing any part of it
in any form without permission. You are supporting writers and allowing
Penguin to continue to publish books for every reader.

The publisher does not have any control over and does not assume any
responsibility for author or third-party websites or their content.

Text copyright © 2018 by Nancy Krulik. Illustrations copyright © 2018
by Ben Balistreri. All rights reserved. Published by Penguin Workshop,
an imprint of Penguin Random House LLC, 345 Hudson Street,
New York, New York 10014. PENGUIN and PENGUIN WORKSHOP
are trademarks of Penguin Books Ltd, and the W colophon is a trademark
of Penguin Random House LLC. Printed in the USA.

Library of Congress Cataloging-in-Publication Data is available.

ISBN 9780515158373 (pbk)   10 9 8 7 6 5 4 3 2 1
ISBN 9780515158380 (hc)   10 9 8 7 6 5 4 3 2 1

NANCY KRULIK

PRINCESS PULVERIZER

Bad moooove!

art by Ben Balistreri

Penguin Workshop
An Imprint of Penguin Random House

For my parents, Gladys and Steve, whose quest for adventure has taken them all over the world—NK

To my third golden retriever, Bombadil. All late-night drawing marathons are better with you by my side—BB

CHAPTER 1

"Cheddar, swiss, and fresh ricotta.
Grilled cheese on rye is a party start-a.
Gouda, brie, and a mild havarti.
Cheese is welcome at any party.
Oh yeah, yeah, yeah. Whoa, whoa, whoa."

Dribble the dragon was happily singing his favorite song as his best friend, Lucas, danced along. They were both in a really good mood this sunny morning.

"I love that song," Lucas said as he kicked his legs and wiggled his hips. *Clink. Clank. Clunk.* His heavy suit of armor set the beat as he danced.

"Me too," Dribble agreed. "Who doesn't love a good cheese song?"

Princess Pulverizer, that's who.

The princess wasn't enjoying Dribble's song at all. She was sitting by the riverbank with her hands clapped over her ears. She had a really sour look on her face. Even more sour than a big hunk of Tyrolean gray cheese.

But Dribble and Lucas weren't about to let a grumpy princess stop their fun. So Dribble kept singing. And Lucas kept dancing.

"Roquefort, taleggio, and a smelly blue.
The stinkier the better, they say that's true."

"Will you cut that out?!" Princess Pulverizer shouted angrily.

Dribble stopped singing.

Lucas stopped dancing.

They both stared at her.

"Come on," Dribble said, trying to urge the princess out of her bad mood. "It's a gorgeous day. The birds are tweeting. The crickets are chirping. *Everyone's* singing."

"And you're *all* making me nuts,"

Princess Pulverizer replied.

"Why are you in such a lousy mood?" Lucas asked the princess.

"Because we're just sitting here, doing nothing," Princess Pulverizer told him.

"No we're not," Lucas insisted. "Dribble is singing. And I'm dancing."

"BUT YOU'RE NOT *SUPPOSED* TO BE SINGING AND DANCING," Princess Pulverizer shouted. "We are supposed to be out there helping people. That's what a Quest of Kindness is all about."

"Oh, *that* again." Dribble groaned.

"Yes, *that* again," Princess Pulverizer told him. "We haven't helped anyone since we freed Lester the Jester from the clutches of the evil Wizard of Wurst."

"That's because we haven't come across anyone in trouble," Lucas said. "Which, if you think about it, is a good thing."

"No it's not," Princess Pulverizer asserted.

Dribble and Lucas stared at her.

"I didn't mean it like that," Princess Pulverizer explained. "I don't like seeing people in trouble. But I really do need to find someone to save. You guys understand that, don't you?"

Dribble and Lucas both nodded. They understood exactly what she meant.

Princess Pulverizer wasn't your average princess. She didn't want to dance the saltarello at royal balls, sip tea with her pinkie in the air at fancy lunches, or balance a heavy crown on top of her head as she welcomed princes into her castle.

That was because Princess Pulverizer didn't want to *be* a princess.

She wanted to be a *knight*. A full-fledged, horseback-riding, armor-wearing, damsel-in-distress-saving kind of knight.

And to do that, she would have to go to Knight School.

Her father, King Alexander, had actually said she could go—on one condition. She had to complete eight good deeds on a Quest of Kindness. Once she had done that, she could get her first set of armor and enter Knight School.

King Alexander had explained that knights were selfless people who spent their lives helping others. A Quest of Kindness would teach Princess Pulverizer to care about other people, the way all good knights did.

So now Princess Pulverizer was traveling the countryside trying to find folks who needed her help. She really, really, *really* wanted to take her place among King Alexander's Knights of the Skround Table.

But doing good deeds was hard work. Luckily for the princess, she had stumbled upon Dribble and Lucas. They were a great help to her, which might surprise a lot of people. After all, Lucas was such a fraidy-cat that the other boys had nicknamed him Lucas the Lily-Livered and laughed him out of Knight School. And Dribble had been banished from his lair because, unlike other dragons, he used his fire for making grilled cheese sandwiches rather than burning down villages.

But Dribble and Lucas were a lot smarter and tougher than they seemed. The princess and her pals had already used their combined talents to defeat two very tough enemies. Unfortunately, that still left six good deeds to go before Princess Pulverizer could return home with eight tokens in hand.

Princess Pulverizer was not exactly known for her patience.

"Someone who needs our help will come along eventually," Dribble assured her. "But for now, let's enjoy this beautiful day." He began singing again.

"*Cheddar.*"

Lucas twirled onto a long, thick log that was sticking way out into the river.

"*Swiss.*"

Lucas whirled around in a circle.

"*And fresh ricotta . . .*"

SPLASH! Lucas twirled and whirled his way off the log and right into the river.

"HELP!" Lucas shouted as he struggled to keep his head above water. "HELP!"

"His armor is weighing him down," Dribble gasped. "He's going to drown!"

"I'll save him!" Princess Pulverizer kicked off her shoes and dived into the water.

She grinned happily as she swam to her friend's aid. Finally, the princess had a good deed to do. Lucas sure was a good pal to fall into the river just to help her out. Any second now she would . . .

Oh no!

Princess Pulverizer looked at Lucas and frowned.

While she had been swimming over to Lucas, Dribble had balanced himself on the long, thick log where Lucas had been dancing and simply *walked* over to where Lucas was bobbing up and down frantically. Now he was holding out his tail like a green safety line.

"Grab on, little buddy," Dribble called to Lucas. "I'll pull you out!"

Princess Pulverizer watched irritably as Lucas grasped the end of Dribble's tail and held on as the dragon dragged him back to shore.

Princess Pulverizer swam back to the riverbank and climbed out of the water. "What did you do that for?" she demanded.

Dribble shrugged. "I couldn't let him drown. He's my best friend."

"I was swimming to him," the princess said. "*I* was supposed to save him."

"You swim too slowly. He would have gone under for good by the time you got there," Dribble told her. "My tail was faster."

It was hard to argue with that.

"Fine," Princess Pulverizer huffed angrily. "But now we have to get going.

I need to find someone *else* to help before the sun goes down."

"Maybe we should wait on that," Lucas suggested.

"Why?" Princess Pulverizer asked impatiently.

"Because you and I stink of fish." Lucas reached into his helmet and pulled out a flip-flopping trout. "Nobody wants to be saved by a smelly knight," he added as he threw the fish back in the water.

Hmmm. He had a point there.

But Princess Pulverizer didn't want to wait for the fishy stink to disappear. That could take a long time. There had to be some way to get rid of the smell.

Out of the corner of her eye, Princess Pulverizer spotted a patch of pretty pink flowers. *Yes! That's it!*

The princess reached down and yanked the pretty posies right out of the ground—roots and all. She shoved a few of them in her hair and a few more into Lucas's visor.

"Now we smell like flowers!" she told Lucas excitedly. "Problem solved."

Dribble wrinkled his snout. "Not exactly. Now you smell like fish *and* flowers."

"It's good enough," Princess Pulverizer said. "Come on. We—"

"BEE!" Lucas shouted, interrupting her and taking off. He tried to outrun a bumblebee that had been resting in one of the flowers Princess Pulverizer had shoved in his helmet. "GET AWAY FROM ME, BEE!"

Princess Pulverizer had never seen Lucas move that quickly. But she was glad he was moving. Now they could finally get on with their quest.

The faster they ran, the faster they could find someone in need of their help.

Of course, if Lucas was way ahead of her, he might stumble across someone to help before she did.

Princess Pulverizer could *not* let that happen.

"Wait for me!" she shouted to Lucas, quickly putting on her boots. "If anyone's gonna save someone, it's gonna be me."

"*Ahem,*" Dribble said, giving her an angry look.

"Oh, right," Princess Pulverizer corrected herself. "I meant wait for Dribble *and* me! Good deeds are easier when you have the power of three!"

CHAPTER 2

RUMBLE! GRUMBLE!

A loud noise filled the village square the trio had just entered. The ground began to shake beneath Princess Pulverizer's feet.

"Earthquake!" Lucas shouted nervously. His skinny legs shook, rattling his armor.

RUMBLE! GRUMBLE!

"I'm getting out of here!" shouted a tall man in a red hat as he covered his head and ran for safety.

"Wait! I'm coming with you!" Lucas cried to the man. He started to run. But Princess Pulverizer grabbed him by the arm and held him in place.

"You're not going anywhere," she told him.

"But the earthquake . . . ," Lucas began.

Princess Pulverizer studied the ground. There were no cracks in the road below her feet. And none of the houses or shops nearby were tilting or crumbling—the way they might if there had really been an earthquake.

So if this isn't an earthquake, what is it? Princess Pulverizer thought nervously to herself.

RUMBLE!
GRUMBLE!

Princess Pulverizer turned around quickly. The noise was definitely coming from behind her. And if she wasn't mistaken, it was coming from inside of something.

Make that inside of some*one*.

"Dribble, it's your stomach making all that noise!" she said.

The dragon's green cheeks blushed purple. "Excuse me," he apologized meekly. "It's not my fault. I'm starving."

"So am I," Lucas admitted. "We haven't eaten in hours."

"No problem," Princess Pulverizer said. "Dribble will just cook up some more of his amazing grilled cheese sandwiches for us."

"No can do," Dribble told the princess.

"Why not?" she asked him.

"We're out of cheese and bread," Dribble replied.

"But we had a whole brick of gouda and a huge loaf of sourdough just yesterday," Princess Pulverizer pointed out.

"We ate it all," Dribble told her. "You had three sandwiches just for lunch."

"Oh right," she admitted. "I forgot. Good thing my father gave me lots of gold and silver pieces before I left on my quest. I'll just buy some more bread and cheese. Problem solved. Easy peasy."

"I can sell you plenty of bread," the old woman who ran the food shop on Old Curds Way told Princess Pulverizer a few minutes later. "But we haven't got any cheese."

"So much for easy peasy," Dribble grumbled. "More like hard as lard."

Lucas gave him a funny look. "Lard isn't hard. It's kind of mushy, actually."

"I only meant that nothing is ever as easy as Princess Pulverizer says it's going to be," Dribble told Lucas.

"Do you know where we can buy some cheese?" Princess Pulverizer asked the shopkeeper.

The old woman stared at Dribble. "Is that a dragon?" she asked nervously.

Princess Pulverizer nodded. "It's okay," she assured her. "He's a nice guy."

"If you say so," the old woman said, moving farther away behind the counter.

"I have a real hankering for some baked brie on sourdough bread," Princess Pulverizer continued. She patted her knapsack. "And I have plenty of gold and silver to buy it with."

"You won't be able to get brie in any store around here," the shopkeeper replied.

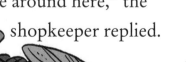

"How about swiss cheese, then?" Lucas suggested. "Or havarti?"

"You can't get cheese anywhere in the village of Ire-Mire-Briar-Shire," the woman told him.

Dribble's eyes grew wide. "No *cheese*?" He gasped. "None at *all*?"

The woman shook her head sadly. "Ire-Mire-Briar-Shire used to be the cheese capital of this whole kingdom. We were overflowing with butter and yogurt, too. But someone has stolen all our cows, goats, and sheep. We have no way to get milk. And without milk, we can't make cheese."

"Hmmm . . . ," Princess Pulverizer mused. "Come to think of it, I haven't heard a single *moo* since we arrived in Ire-Mire-Briar-Shire."

"Or a *baaaa*," Lucas added. "Or a *maaaa*."

"This is an outrage!" Dribble shouted so loudly, the whole shop shook.

The shopkeeper dived to catch a jar of jam as it flew off the shelf.

"Sorry," Dribble apologized. "I just can't believe it."

"I know." The old woman wiped away a tear.

"Do you know what kind of cheese is made backward?" Princess Pulverizer asked the shopkeeper.

"No."

"Edam!" Princess Pulverizer exclaimed.

"Get it? *E-d-a-m*. It's *made* spelled backward."

Lucas, Dribble, and the shopkeeper all stared at her.

"Sheesh, I was just trying to lighten the mood and make everyone feel better," Princess Pulverizer said. "Like any good knight would do."

"A good knight would probably know when and where to make a cheese joke," Dribble scolded her. "There's nothing funny about a village without cheese!"

"Do you have any idea who could have stolen the animals?" Lucas asked.

"No," the shopkeeper admitted. "But it had to be someone who needed a whole lot of cheese. He took every herd we had."

"*GRRRRR!*" Dribble let out an angry growl. "I can't believe it. No dairy!

That means no buttery croissants. No milk to dunk doughnuts in. *No grilled cheese!*"

Dribble was so upset, a spark of fire escaped from his snout as he shouted.

The old woman ducked nervously behind the counter.

"It is a shame," Lucas agreed quietly.

"A SHAME?" Dribble bellowed. "It's more than a shame. It's *UNACCEPTABLE*! Someone has to bring cheese back to Ire-Mire-Briar-Shire. And we're just the ones to do it! Let's go. We have a good deed to do."

"Hey! That's *my* line!" Princess Pulverizer insisted. But she hurried after him anyway, dragging a nervous Lucas behind her.

CHAPTER 3

"Can you see any animals from up there?"
Dribble called to Lucas a few hours later
as the trio traveled along in the hills
outside Ire-Mire-Briar-Shire.

Lucas was perched on the tip of
Dribble's tail, searching the countryside
for the stolen cows, sheep, and goats.
"Not yet," he answered.

"They have to be here somewhere,"
Dribble grumbled. He picked up his pace.

"Whole herds don't just disappear into thin air."

"Slow down," Lucas pleaded with the dragon. "You almost threw me off on that last turn."

"Quit complaining," Princess Pulverizer scolded Lucas. "At least you're getting a ride. I've been walking this whole time. And we are miles and miles from Ire-Mire-Briar-Shire!"

"I almost forgot you were down there," Lucas told her. "I didn't hear your footsteps at all."

"That's because I'm wearing the magical ruby ring that the Queen of Shmergermeister gave us as a thank-you for helping her," Princess Pulverizer explained. "Anyone who wears this ring moves in complete silence."

"Then why can we still hear you talking to us?" asked Dribble.

"The ring only seems to keep my footsteps quiet—not my mouth," the princess replied.

"Well, it definitely works," Lucas told her. "Your feet aren't making a sound."

"No, but they are getting blisters," Princess Pulverizer told Lucas. "This is such a steep hill we're climbing. I wouldn't mind taking a turn riding up there on Dribble's tail."

Lucas didn't reply. Instead, he pointed at some place off in the distance and began bouncing up and down. "There they are!" he shouted. "I can see them! There's a huge herd of animals in that pasture beyond the pine trees!"

Dribble stopped short to stare at the

pasture down below the hill. "We found them!" he shouted excitedly. "We did it!"

"No wonder the people of Ire-Mire-Briar-Shire didn't find them," Lucas said. "It would be hard for someone to see the pasture through these trees if they weren't riding high on a dragon's tail, and standing at the top of this hill."

Princess Pulverizer was thrilled. "That's number three!" she cheered.

"Is that Quest of Kindness all you can think about?" Dribble asked her. "Is it all about what *you* can get out of this?"

"I . . . well . . . um . . . *no*," Princess Pulverizer answered. "I meant there are *three* different kinds of animals out there *for* us to bring back—cows, sheep, and goats. To help the people of Ire-Mire-Briar-Shire."

Dribble gave her a funny look.

"Speaking of the Quest of Kindness," Lucas said. "We actually haven't really done anything to help the people of Ire-Mire-Briar-Shire yet."

"What are you talking about?" Princess Pulverizer demanded. "We found their animals."

"Yes," Lucas agreed. "But now we have to figure out how to get them all the way from here back to there."

"He's right. We have to herd them back to the village," Dribble agreed. He looked at the princess. "Do you know how to herd animals?"

"Well, no," Princess Pulverizer admitted. "But how hard can herding be? I mean, German shepherds do it all the time. If a dog can do it, a human can."

"Excuse me?" Dribble was so angry, his whole body shook.

"Whoa!" Lucas shouted.

Clank! The knight-in-training fell from the top of the dragon's tail.

"Ow! That hurt!" Lucas exclaimed.

"Sorry," Dribble apologized. "She just makes me so mad."

"What did I say?" Princess Pulverizer asked him.

"Why do you think that humans are so much better than everyone else?" Dribble demanded. "You act like you're the big cheese, but you're not. You know, dragons can do a lot of things humans can't, like breathe fire and fly."

"You can't fly," Princess Pulverizer countered.

"Not yet," Dribble admitted. "But as soon as my big, grown-up wings grow in, I'll be able to."

"Please stop fighting," Lucas said as he scrambled to his feet and hurried to stand between them. "We're all just really hangry right now."

"Hangry?" Princess Pulverizer and Dribble asked at the same time.

"You know, when you're angry because you're hungry," Lucas explained. "We need to work together and focus on getting these animals back to town."

"Exactly," Princess Pulverizer said. "I'm going to show both of you how easy it is."

The princess hurried down the hill, dodging between the thick pines and taking care not to slide in the mud. Finally, she reached the clearing that formed the pasture where the animals were busy eating. She climbed over the fence and ran toward a group of cows happily munching on some grass.

"Move it," she shouted at the cows.

One cow glanced up in her direction and blinked. The others ignored her completely.

WHOA! WHAT?

No one ignored Princess Pulverizer! It just wasn't done. Unless . . .

Maybe they didn't understand her. After all, they *were* cows.

The princess was simply going to have to speak cow. "*Moooo*ve it!" she shouted again.

But the cows didn't move. They just stood there, eating.

Which made Princess Pulverizer's empty stomach rumble. Those cows were very rude, eating in front of a hungry person like that.

"*MOOOOOOOOOOOOOOOVE IT!*" she bellowed angrily.

The cows stopped eating for a moment. They turned their backs on her.

And if she wasn't mistaken, Princess Pulverizer thought she heard one of them laughing.

No, wait. That wasn't a *cow* laughing. That was a *dragon* laughing. Dribble was hooting and snorting so hard, he was doubled over and rolling around on the ground.

"So you can do anything a dog can, huh?" he called out to her.

Grrrrr. Now Princess Pulverizer was really mad.

"I just have to figure out a way to get the cows to understand me," she said as she tramped her way back out of the pasture. "And I will. But I can't think when I'm this hungry. And thirsty."

"Well, we can at least have some milk," Lucas told her.

"You have milk?" Princess Pulverizer asked him.

"No, but *they* do," Lucas said, pointing at the cows, sheep, and goats in the meadow. "All we have to do is fill our water bougets with their milk," he said, holding up the leather pouch he usually filled with drinking water.

"Good idea!" Princess Pulverizer said to him. "You and Dribble go milk a few cows. The milk will give me the energy to come up with a plan to herd the animals."

"Okay," Lucas agreed. He started to walk toward the pasture.

"Wait a minute," Dribble said.

"Okay," Lucas agreed again. He stopped walking.

"What's the problem?" Princess Pulverizer asked the dragon.

"*You're* the problem," Dribble told her. "How come Lucas and I have to do all the milking while you just sit there?"

"I'm not just sitting," Princess Pulverizer countered. "I'm thinking."

"Well, how about *I* think, while *you* milk?" Dribble asked her.

"Princesses do not milk," Princess Pulverizer explained.

"But you don't want to be a princess," Dribble reminded her. "You want to be a knight. And knights always do whatever

‹44›

it takes to get the job done."

It was hard to argue with that. "Fine," Princess Pulverizer said. "Come on, Lucas."

"Maybe we should leave our swords behind with Dribble," Lucas suggested. "The sight of a sharp sword might scare the animals away."

Princess Pulverizer sighed. She didn't think animals were scared of swords. But you never knew. And besides, she was too hungry and thirsty to argue with Lucas. So she pulled her sword out and handed it to Dribble.

"Don't worry, I'll keep it safe," the dragon assured her. "I'll be right over there, behind those trees. It looks like a nice shady spot to take a milk break."

"Have you ever milked anything

before?" Lucas asked Princess Pulverizer
as he removed his sword.

"Sure, lots of times," Princess Pulverizer
told him.

Suddenly, the sword began to shake
vigorously in Dribble's hands.

"Liar," Dribble said.

"I'm not lying," Princess
Pulverizer argued. "I have . . ."

She stopped midsentence and stared
at the shaking sword. She had forgotten
that when the King of Salamistonia had

given it to her as a token of his gratitude for bringing laughter back to his kingdom, he had explained that the magical sword could always tell when someone was lying.

"All you have to do is point it directly at someone," the king had explained. "If he is telling the truth, the sword will remain still. But if he is lying, it will begin to quiver."

And boy was it quivering now.

"Okay, so I've never actually milked anything," Princess Pulverizer admitted. "But I've *seen* people do it."

With that, the princess climbed back over the fence and into the pasture. She was determined to fill her leather pouch with plenty of fresh milk. Because Dribble would never let her live it down if this milking mission turned out to be an *udder* failure.

CHAPTER 4

"I think you pull on these things under here and the milk comes right out," Princess Pulverizer told Lucas.

Lucas stuck his head under a sheep and pulled. "Hey!" he exclaimed as a big squirt of sheep milk hit him right in the eye.

"I think you figured it out," Princess Pulverizer told him. She started laughing.

Lucas frowned. "Don't laugh at me," he said sadly. "It's not nice."

"Come on," Princess Pulverizer said. "It was funny."

Lucas shrugged. "Maybe a *little* funny."

"It sure is taking a long time to fill this pouch," Princess Pulverizer said as she milked a cow.

"Yeah, but it will be worth it," Lucas told her. "There's nothing like fresh milk."

"Too bad we forgot to buy some bread while we were in Ire-Mire-Briar-Shire," Princess Pulverizer said. "It would be great to dunk a hunk of pumpernickel."

"Or a thick sourdough . . . ," Lucas suggested.

Lucas and Princess Pulverizer were so busy talking about all the kinds of bread that could be dunked into fresh milk, they didn't notice the looming shadow overhead.

"Once we bring all these animals back to Ire-Mire-Briar-Shire, they will be able to make all sorts of cheeses," Princess Pulverizer continued.

Just then a thick black net cascaded onto her head!

"WHOA!" the princess exclaimed. She began twisting and turning, trying to free herself. "Hey, let us out of this thing!"

But whoever had captured her was not letting go. In fact, he pulled the net tighter around them.

Princess Pulverizer looked up through the netting to get a glimpse of her captor. At first, all she saw was the inside of a massive nose. Two cavernous nostrils twitched over her head. She sure hoped this big guy wasn't about to sneeze!

The princess twisted her neck back a bit to get a look at the face that went with the nose. The huge creature had bulging brown eyes, which were open so wide, they looked as though they might pop right out of his head. He had a mole on his chin, and another on the tip of his nose.

But the most striking thing about him was
the shock of pink hair on top of his head.
It looked like a
giant pink
haystack.

Princess Pulverizer had only ever heard
of one kind of creature with hair like that.

A *troll*.

Princess Pulverizer had read stories
about the trolls that hid in the pine forests
in neighboring kingdoms. But none of
those stories had mentioned how big a
troll could be. Or how hideous.

This troll was seriously ugly. And
seriously angry.

"Gotcha!" the troll bellowed
triumphantly. "Nobody steals milk from
my cows and gets away with it."

"HELP!" Lucas cried out. "DRIBBLE,
HELP!"

Lucas was shouting at the top of his
lungs. But his dragon pal was too far away
to hear him.

"Don't worry," Princess Pulverizer

assured her friend. "I'll just cut us out
of this net."

The princess reached for her sword.

Uh-oh. She'd left her sword with
Dribble. She *couldn't* cut a hole in the
netting. Talk about a bad moooove . . .

Sob. Sob. SOB. Lucas started crying.
Princess Pulverizer couldn't stand the
sound of Lucas's sobs. They were so loud.
And pitiful. She wished he would just
stop.

SOB! SOB!
SOBBBBB!

Or maybe she didn't wish he'd stop at all. Surely Dribble had heard that last cry. People in the next three kingdoms could have heard that last cry.

Any minute now, their big green buddy would come running to their rescue.

SOOOOBBBBBBB!

But Dribble didn't come.

Princess Pulverizer was confused. How could the dragon not have heard that?

He was probably singing one of his dumb songs so loudly that he drowned out the sound of the sobbing.

And if that was the case, there was only one thing left to do. Princess Pulverizer was going to have to tear a hole in the net with her bare hands.

The princess reached out and grabbed the thick black netting.

She pulled at it.

She punched at it.

She *pulverized* it.

But the netting didn't tear. Not one tiny inch.

SOB! SOB! SOB! Lucas just kept on crying.

"You may as well stop struggling," the pink-haired troll bellowed at the princess. "You two are my prisoners now. There is no escaping."

Thump.

Bump.

Clank.

The troll opened the top of the net and spilled Princess Pulverizer and Lucas out onto the cold, hard floor.

"Welcome to my cave," the troll said in an eerie voice.

Princess Pulverizer felt her stomach flip-flop. She hated to admit it, but she was scared. This troll was clearly a mean guy. Somehow she had a feeling he hadn't brought them to his home for a nice visit and a cup of tea.

"It's cold in here," Lucas whimpered. "And dark. I hate the dark."

Princess Pulverizer wasn't too fond of the dark, either. But she didn't tell Lucas that. She needed to at least *pretend* she wasn't scared. She'd heard the knights who sat around her father's Skround Table say the same thing a million times: "Never let your enemies see you sweat."

It wasn't easy pretending to be brave. Especially with all the creepy crawling creatures that were lingering at her legs and slithering around her sides. It was too dark to see what they were, but spiders and snakes were a pretty good guess.

"Stay put!" the troll told Princess Pulverizer and Lucas. "Don't move a muscle. *Or else.*"

In the darkness, Princess Pulverizer heard the troll's heavy footsteps walking away from her. She could tell he was walking toward the glow of sunlight in the distance.

That was clearly where the opening of the cave was. If they were going to escape, they were going to have to make their way to that light.

SQUAWROARK!

Yikes! The sudden loud noise made Princess Pulverizer jump.

"What was that?" Lucas asked her nervously.

"I don't know," Princess Pulverizer admitted. "It sounded like some sort of animal."

"I never heard an animal make a noise like that," Lucas said.

"Me either," Princess Pulverizer told him. "But it was coming from the opening of the cave." She pulled Lucas to his feet. "Come on. We have to see what's going on."

"The troll told us not to move a muscle. Or else," Lucas fretted.

"He didn't say or else *what*," Princess Pulverizer told him. "Maybe he meant 'or else I won't be able to give you the big gift I have for you.' Maybe he's nicer than he sounds."

"I doubt that was it," Lucas said.

Princess Pulverizer doubted that, too.

But she had to get Lucas to move somehow. "Come on," she told him. "We can't just sit here."

"But he'll hear us if we move," Lucas said. "My armor clanks. And you walk so hard on your heels."

"I do not," Princess Pulverizer said.

"You do," Lucas said. "You sound like an elephant when you walk."

Princess Pulverizer frowned. She knew it was the truth. Lady Frump, her teacher at the school of manners, told her that all the time. She twirled her ruby ring nervously.

Wait! That was it! *The ruby ring.*

"The magic ring will let us walk without a sound," she reminded Lucas.

"That's good for you," Lucas said. "But *I'll* still be clanking."

"Hold my hand," Princess Pulverizer told him. "And make sure your fingers are touching the ruby. That will keep you quiet, too. And whatever you do, don't let go."

Lucas did as he was told. He held on to the princess's hand. Tight. So tight that she thought the blood had stopped flowing to her fingers. Wow. For a lily-livered scaredy-cat, Lucas sure was strong.

As they walked in complete silence toward the mouth of the cave, the light became stronger. And that's when Princess Pulverizer got her first glimpse of the creature that had made the bloodcurdling sound. It had the body of a lion and the head and the wings of an eagle.

It's a griffin, Princess Pulverizer thought. *Fascinating.*

Princess Pulverizer had seen drawings of griffins on the shields of some of the royal Knights of the Skround Table. But she'd never seen one in person.

"Wait until you see what I caught us for dinner tonight," Princess Pulverizer heard the troll tell the griffin. "I'm thinking we'll start off with a hot bowl of princess-and-potato soup, followed by a knight-and-nutmeg casserole."

"Did you hear that?" Lucas whispered nervously. He began to whimper.

Princess Pulverizer slapped her
free hand over his mouth.
"Shhhh," she warned.

"Or better yet, how about a double-decker princess-knight sandwich?" the terrifying troll suggested.

"*Squawroark,*" the griffin replied.

"Yes! That's perfect," the troll said. "I'm going to head into the garden to get some lettuce and tomato for our sandwiches. Gotta eat those veggies, you know."

"*Squawroark,*" the griffin repeated.

"You guard the prisoners," the pink-haired troll ordered the griffin. "And when I get back, we'll cook them up just the way we like them—medium rare."

CHAPTER 5

"Did you hear that?" Lucas whispered. "He's going to cook us and eat us with lettuce and tomatoes."

"I heard him," Princess Pulverizer replied.

"We've got to get out of here," Lucas whimpered.

Princess Pulverizer looked up. The griffin was perched on a ledge near the mouth of the cave. His sharp eagle eyes would surely spot them trying to sneak out. And with his lionlike strength, there would be no defeating him when he did. Especially since they no longer had their swords.

"I have no idea how to get past him," the princess admitted.

"What do you mean you have no idea?" Lucas asked her. "You *always* have an idea."

"Why am I the one who has to come up with an idea?" Princess Pulverizer demanded. "*You* come up with one."

"Well . . . um . . . we could . . . ," Lucas stammered.

"Not so easy, is it?" Princess Pulverizer asked him.

Lucas shook his head and let out a little cry.

"We can't keep arguing," Princess Pulverizer told him. "We have to stick together if we're going to get out of here and rescue those animals."

"There sure were a lot of cows, sheep, and goats in that pasture. Why does the troll need so many? Unless . . ." Lucas gulped and started to shake.

"Unless what?" Princess Pulverizer demanded.

"Unless there's a whole *army* of trolls out there who drink a lot of milk. Or a mob of angry griffins who like cheese," Lucas said. "It's just the two of us here. We can't get past a whole army." He started to cry again.

Princess Pulverizer didn't blame him.

She felt like crying herself.

Princess Pulverizer was not the type of person to give up. But here they were, just she and Lucas. With no weapons to—

THUMP. THUMP. THUMP. THUMP.

Suddenly the ground began to shake.

Princess Pulverizer gasped. Lucas was right!

"It sounds like a whole army!" she exclaimed.

"*SQUAWROARK!*" The griffin let out a loud cry. Even he sounded fearful.

Surprisingly, Lucas *wasn't* afraid. "I know those footsteps," he said happily. "That's Dribble. He's come to save us."

THUMP. THUMP. THUMP. THUMP.

The dragon's footsteps grew closer. Then they stopped short.

"Hi there," Princess Pulverizer heard Dribble say. He didn't sound very far away. But who was he talking to?

"I was wondering," Dribble continued. "Have you seen a young knight-in-training and a princess who wants to be a knight-in-training?"

"Nope."

That reply came from the troll. Princess Pulverizer would recognize his eerie voice anywhere.

Princess Pulverizer gave a slight sigh of relief. Dribble must have stopped the troll before he could reach his garden. That was good news. Because if Dribble could just keep the troll talking for a while, it might give her enough time to think of a plan.

"There's nobody here except my griffin and me," the troll told Dribble.

"We—" Lucas started to cry out to his friend. But Princess Pulverizer clapped her hand over his mouth and pointed up to where the griffin was perched.

"If the troll hears you, he'll sic the griffin on us before Dribble can do a thing!" Princess Pulverizer whispered into Lucas's ear.

Lucas took one look at the griffin's sharp claws and sealed his mouth shut.

"Are you sure?" Dribble asked.

"Sure, I'm sure," the troll said. "I haven't seen anyone."

"Are you lying?" Dribble asked him.

"Why would I do that?" the troll asked him. "I'm telling you. No princess. No knight. Just the griffin and me."

"YOU ARE LYING!" Dribble bellowed. "They're around here somewhere and I'm going to find them."

"I have better things to do than argue with you," the troll said. "I have vegetables to pick."

Princess Pulverizer listened as the troll's footsteps grew farther and farther away.

"Hey! I'm not done talking to you yet!" Dribble shouted after him. "Where are my friends?"

But the troll didn't answer.

And a moment later, Dribble *thump-thump*ed away, too. Princess Pulverizer and Lucas huddled together, whispering.

"Well, I gotta say, that troll is pretty brave," Princess Pulverizer admitted. "Most folks are scared of dragons."

"Maybe he's brave because he's got a whole army at his command," Lucas suggested.

"Don't start that again," Princess Pulverizer warned him. "We don't know that he has an army."

"We don't know that he *doesn't* have one, either," Lucas countered.

Princess Pulverizer frowned. He had her there.

The princess didn't want to talk about armies anymore. "Let's change the subject," she said. "Talk about anything else."

"How about Dribble?" Lucas suggested. "He sure is smart. I don't know how he figured out the troll was lying."

"He's got the magic sword," Princess Pulverizer reminded him. "It must have been quivering like mad when that troll lied about having seen us."

"Oh right," Lucas said. "And Dribble knows that sword is never wrong. He's not going to go off somewhere searching for us. He's going to stay nearby. He'll find us and rescue us. He's the bravest creature I know."

Princess Pulverizer shot Lucas a look.

"I mean other than you, of course," Lucas corrected himself. "But you're in here. And Dribble is out there."

Princess Pulverizer sighed. Dribble was out there. All alone.

Or *not* all alone. There was no telling what the troll was hiding up his sleeve.

But whatever it was, it wasn't good for Dribble. He would need the power of three to fight whatever evil was lurking around. She and Lucas had to get out of this cave. And fast.

But how?

CHAPTER 6

Princess Pulverizer was thinking. And pacing.

Back and forth.

Back and forth.

As she paced, she was aware of the griffin's eagle eyes. He was staring straight down at her—keeping track of her every move.

Back and forth.

Back and—ZZZ . . . ZZZZ . . .

"What was that?" the princess asked nervously.

"Shhh . . . ," Lucas warned her. He pointed up toward the ledge outside the cave.

Princess Pulverizer looked up. It was the griffin. He was almost asleep.

"Griffins snore?!" Princess Pulverizer exclaimed. "That's a surprise!"

The sound of her voice woke the griffin. His yellow eyes opened wide. He glared at her angrily.

"Oops," the princess said in a much quieter voice.

She began thinking and pacing again.

Back and forth.

Back and forth.

"He's getting sleepy," Lucas whispered as the princess paced. "His eyes are droopy. I wonder why."

The princess shrugged. "No idea," she said, stopping her pacing long enough to wipe her brow. The light coming from the mouth of the cave reflected off the giant ruby on her finger.

The griffin's eyes shot open at the sight of the bright red light.

"It's the ring!" Lucas whispered excitedly. He pointed to the princess's left hand. The light was reflecting off the big red ruby. "He's watching your ring while you move. It's hypnotizing him."

Hypnotizing? Is it possible?

"You know, one time a hypnotist came to our palace to put on a show," Princess Pulverizer told Lucas. "He hypnotized the Prince of Fergerberger. Every time a bell rang, the prince barked like a dog and tried to chase his tail."

SQUAWROARK!

Uh-oh. The griffin was *wide* awake now.

"Start pacing again," Lucas begged the princess.

Princess Pulverizer did not like to be told what to do. *She* was the one who was supposed to give the orders. After all, she was the Royal Princess of Empiria and—

SQUAWROARK!

Okay, maybe I'll take orders this one time, Princess Pulverizer thought. *That griffin is one dangerous creature.*

The princess began pacing again, making sure the light hit the ring as she swung her arms back and forth.

"You are getting sleepy," Princess Pulverizer said in a soft, soothing voice. Well, at least as soft and soothing as she could manage. Princess Pulverizer was not a soft, soothing kind of girl.

ZZZZZZZ. ZZZZZZZ. ZZZZZZZZZZZZZZZZ.

Princess Pulverizer smiled to herself.

She had managed to outwit a griffin. The big lion-bird was sleeping like a baby. But for how long?

Princess Pulverizer wasn't about to wait around and find out. "Quick," she whispered, grabbing Lucas and pulling him out of the cave. "Now's our chance!"

CHAPTER 7

It seemed to Princess Pulverizer that she had been running for hours. She could barely breathe as she darted among the trees, trying to avoid leaving a straight path of footprints that the troll could follow.

Lucas was right behind her. He was moving quickly, which was pretty impressive considering he was wearing his suit of armor.

Finally, when she didn't think she could take another step, Princess Pulverizer stopped running. She put her hands on her knees, bent over, and tried to catch her breath.

"I think we're safe here," she told Lucas. "That troll will have a hard time finding us in this deep dark part of the forest."

"So will Dribble," Lucas pointed out sadly. He took a deep breath and looked around. "He's never going to find us here."

"Then we'll have to find him," Princess Pulverizer said, trying to sound confident. But she wasn't confident at all. They had been running quite a while. And so far they hadn't seen a single sign of the big guy.

"I'm getting worried," Lucas said. "Dribble would never travel far if he thought we were still around here. What if he was captured and dragged off?"

Lucas was starting to panic. Princess Pulverizer had to get him thinking about something else. Luckily, the perfect thing was right under her nose.

"Boy, something sure stinks out here," Princess Pulverizer remarked. "A forest should smell like pine trees and flowers. But *this* forest smells awful."

Lucas didn't answer. Instead he gulped. And shook. And pointed his finger over the princess's shoulder.

"Ch-ch-cheese monster," he stammered nervously.

"You mean muenster cheese?" Princess Pulverizer corrected him. "No, I don't think that's what it is. Muenster cheese isn't usually this stinky."

Lucas shook his head, hard. "Ch-ch-cheese *monster*," he stammered again. "O-o-over th-th-there."

Princess Pulverizer whipped around to see what Lucas was pointing at.

And that's when she saw him: a massive monster made completely of cheese!

Gulp.

Princess Pulverizer looked up—*way* up—into the monster's crumbly blue-cheese eyes.

The monster glared down at Princess Pulverizer.

Princess Pulverizer did not turn away. She didn't even blink. The princess was a champion at staring contests. Not one girl at Lady Frump's Royal School of Ladylike Manners had ever beaten her.

So she kept staring.

And the monster kept glaring.

Zzzap . . .

Just then, a hungry fly landed on the Cheese Monster's cheek. The monster swatted it away and then scratched at his face. One of the holes in his swiss cheese cheek stretched wide, and a glob of cream cheese oozed down the side of his face.

"Gross!" Lucas gulped and ran off to hide behind a pine tree.

Princess Pulverizer thought about hiding, too. But she didn't. Because real knights didn't hide from danger.

But real knights had swords to fight with. Princess Pulverizer had nothing but her fists. Strong as she was, the princess was no match for that monster's massive mozzarella muscles.

The monster shook his head angrily. Ropes of his string-cheese hair flipped and flopped all around. Flakes of parmesan dandruff fell from his head and drifted to the ground like stinky, smelly snowflakes.

AAARRGGG! The monster opened his mouth and let out a frightening growl.

Princess Pulverizer jumped back. Boy, that monster had bad breath. Which wasn't surprising, seeing as his shoulders, neck, and armpits were all sculpted from limburger cheese—the smelliest cheese of all.

No wonder the troll needed all those cows, sheep, and goats, Princess Pulverizer thought. It took a whole lot of cheese to build a giant monster.

And no wonder the troll wasn't afraid of Dribble. A dragon who still had his baby wings would be no match for this monstrous mound of cheese.

But that still left one big question unanswered: Why would the pink-haired troll need a cheese monster, anyway?

AAARRGGG! The monster let out another growl. The smell of limburger cheese wafted out of his mouth.

A flock of birds flew off.

A scurry of chipmunks scampered away.

And a gaze of raccoons hid in a group of hollow logs.

Princess Pulverizer didn't blame the animals for getting out of there. Who wouldn't run away from that smell?

"CHEESE! I SMELL CHEESE!"

Dribble. That's who.

The big green dragon was racing toward her at top speed. His tiny wings were flapping excitedly, and there was a massive smile on his face.

"CHEESE!" the dragon shouted again.

"Dribble's here!" Lucas cheered from his hiding spot. "He's come to help us."

Princess Pulverizer hurried over to Dribble. "Boy, am I glad to see you," she said, grabbing her sword from his claw.

Princess Pulverizer was feeling brave now. She, Lucas, and Dribble would soon be fighting together.

The power of three was the best weapon of all!

CHAPTER 8

"Take that!" Princess Pulverizer shouted as she lunged at the Cheese Monster.

But before the tip of her sword could puncture even an inch of the monster's cheesy body, he swung his massive arm into a thick-trunked pine tree.

Thwack.

Uh-oh. The monster had cut the trunk clear through.

Crack.

The giant tree began to teeter toward the ground. Princess Pulverizer leaped backward and out of the way to keep from getting smooshed.

Clunk.

The tree slammed to the ground, separating the princess from her pals.

AAARRGGG! The monster let out a bloodcurdling cry.

"I wish he'd stop doing that," the princess heard Lucas whimper nervously.

Princess Pulverizer wasn't frightened by the monster's shout. (Okay, maybe she was. But there was no way she was letting her fear keep her from fighting!) Immediately, she tried climbing over the tree trunk. It wasn't easy, seeing as the thick trunk was as high as her shoulders. No matter how she tried, the princess just couldn't pull herself up.

Well, if I can't go over it, I'll just go around it, Princess Pulverizer thought. Quickly she darted over to the tip of the fallen tree.

"Ow!" Princess Pulverizer exclaimed as she ran right into a thick bush full of thorns.

The fallen tree was surrounded on either end by the prickly bushes. There was no getting through them. She would come out the other side looking like grated cheese.

Just then Princess Pulverizer heard Dribble cry out, "I've had enough!"

AAAARRRG! the monster growled. He sounded furious.

"WHOA!" Dribble yelped. This time his voice was coming from high in the sky.

Princess Pulverizer looked up to see the monster's huge havarti hand holding Dribble by the tail. He started spinning Dribble around and around in midair.

"I'm getting dizzy!" Dribble shouted.

The Cheese Monster whirled Dribble harder and harder. And then . . .

THUD!

Princess Pulverizer stood on her tiptoes and peered over the fallen tree trunk just in time to see the monster drop Dribble right on his bright green dragon bottom.

"Everything's spinning." Dribble groaned, gripping his stomach. "I don't feel so good . . . *blech*."

Well, that was a surprise! Who knew dragon puke was purple?

"Nobody makes my friend throw up!" Princess Pulverizer heard Lucas shout. "Not even a big, scary, smelly cheese monster."

Princess Pulverizer craned her neck to see what was happening. She watched in amazement as Lucas leaped out from his hiding place, grabbed his sword from Dribble, and charged at the monster.

Princess Pulverizer stared at Lucas. All of a sudden, the timid guy looked like a knight. A real live, very brave knight.

But only for a moment.

CLANK. Lucas's visor slammed shut.

"Hey!" he shouted. "Who turned out the lights?"

Aarrghhh hee hee. The monster roared again. Only this time, it sounded like he was laughing. He scooped Lucas up in his giant hand and held him high in the air.

Aarrghhh hee hee.

"Stop laughing at me," Lucas grumbled. His feelings were hurt.

But the monster didn't care about Lucas's feelings.

Aarrghhh hee hee. He laughed again.

Then he yanked a few long, thick strands of string-cheese hair from his head and used them to tie Lucas to a tree.

Lucas twisted right. He twisted left. But he could not break free.

"That's some strong string cheese," Dribble said with surprise. "Must be made with heavy cream!"

Princess Pulverizer frowned. It was clear Dribble and Lucas weren't going to be any help at this point. It would be up to her to defeat the giant monster.

And there was no way she was letting a little thing like a huge fallen tree trunk get in her way.

There might not be any way she could climb over the trunk. But that didn't mean she couldn't *fly* over it.

Well, sort of fly, anyway.

While the monster was busy cheering for himself, Princess Pulverizer began climbing the branches of a nearby tree. She climbed higher and higher. When she'd gotten as far up as she could, Princess Pulverizer looked down.

Bad move.

The ground was very, very far away. If she didn't time this just right, or if she landed wrong . . .

No! Princess Pulverizer couldn't think about that now. She couldn't think at all. She had to just . . .

JUMP!

For a moment, time seemed to stop.

All Princess Pulverizer could feel was her body falling straight down. Because no matter how smart or how strong they might be, princesses cannot fly.

Princess Pulverizer felt herself picking up speed. The ground was getting closer and closer. She closed her eyes in fear.

She was falling . . . falling . . .

THUMP!

Princess Pulverizer landed right on top of the Cheese Monster's smelly shoulders.

She opened her eyes and smiled.

Yes! A perfect landing!

Aarrghhhh! The monster shouted and leaped backward with surprise.

He reached behind him, trying to push the princess to the ground. But she grabbed his neck and held on tight.

The Cheese Monster turned to the left.

He turned to the right.

He spun around in a circle. But he could not shake Princess Pulverizer, no matter how hard he tried.

Princess Pulverizer stabbed her sword into the Cheese Monster's back. She poked at his arms. She sliced his rear end.

But nothing hurt him.

Clearly, it was going to take a lot more than a sword to stop this guy. Princess Pulverizer wasn't going to be able to beat him alone. Quickly, she shinnied down the Cheese Monster's back and raced over to Lucas. With a single swish of her sword, she cut him free.

"Thanks," Lucas said, lifting his visor so he could see.

AAARRRGHHHHHHHHHHH!!!!!! The monster let out a mighty roar.

"AAHH!" Lucas cried back in fear.

"That monster is getting stronger," Dribble told Princess Pulverizer. "There's no way we can defeat him."

Princess Pulverizer frowned. Dribble was right. The madder the monster got, the stronger he became. And he was really furious. His blue-cheese eyes had closed into angry little slits. His mozzarella muscles were flexed and ready for battle. And his feta cheese feet were planted firmly on the ground.

Wait a minute.

Princess Pulverizer looked back down at the monster's huge feet. There was a puddle of sticky stuff forming around his toes. Which gave Princess Pulverizer a great idea.

Maybe there *was* a way to defeat the Cheese Monster after all!

CHapter 9

The Cheese Monster had done the one thing the Knights of the Skround Table were warned never to do—he'd let his enemies see him sweat. Stinky, slimy, *cheesy* sweat!

That growing puddle around the monster's feet was actually melted cheese. The more the monster moved around in the hot sun, the more his cheesy body dissolved.

But the monster was huge. At this rate it would take days, even weeks, to get him to melt away. And the pink-haired troll would be back soon.

Princess Pulverizer had to rush this melting thing along. Somehow she had to raise the temperature around here.

But how?

"Dribble!" she cried out suddenly. "Breathe fire!"

Dribble looked at her in shock. "Breathe what?" he asked her.

"Fire!" she repeated. "You have to shoot your flames at the monster."

"You know I don't use my fire to hurt anyone," Dribble reminded her. "That's why the other dragons threw me out of our lair."

"This isn't any*one*," Princess Pulverizer insisted. "It's just a big mound of cheese. And when you grill the bread to make sandwiches, the cheese melts, doesn't it?"

"I guess so," Dribble agreed.

"Then start grilling," Princess Pulverizer told him.

"Well, when you put it that way," Dribble replied. He took a deep breath, opened his mouth, and let out a roaring flame.

Almost instantly, the monster's knees began to melt down into his ankles.

"It's working!" Princess Pulverizer shouted excitedly.

The smell of smoked cheese filled the air.

"Yum!" Dribble said. He blew a heavy flame right at the monster's arm. His mozzarella muscles melted. "I love smoked mozzarella."

So did Princess Pulverizer. The smell was making her hungry—until Dribble aimed a fiery flame at the Cheese Monster's belly.

"Oh, yuck!" Lucas exclaimed. "Smoked limburger cheese actually smells worse than regular limburger cheese."

Princess Pulverizer had to agree. The air around her was starting to stink. She held her nose and tried to breathe through her mouth.

"Come on, Dribble. Breathe harder," she said. "We gotta get out of here."

"I'm doing the best I can," Dribble told her.

It wouldn't be long before the griffin would awaken from his nap and alert the troll that his prisoners had escaped. Princess Pulverizer had to speed things up.

Quickly, she grabbed Lucas and turned him toward the sun. The hot rays bounced off his metal armor and up toward the monster's neck.

Aarrrggghhhh! The monster tried to lunge toward the princess. But his legs had already melted away. And his arms were shrinking by the second.

"Help me, Lucas," Princess Pulverizer called out. "Make this guy really sweat!"

Lucas jumped into action, running in circles around the melting monster. The Cheese Monster turned his body around and around, trying to catch the knight-in-training. And the more the monster turned, the more he sweat.

"It's working!" Princess Pulverizer cheered. The monster was now nothing more than a head made of swiss cheese floating in a sea of melted monster mush.

"WHAT'S GOING ON HERE?!"

Princess Pulverizer stopped cheering. She would know that voice anywhere. It was the pink-haired troll. He was back. And he was *angry*!

"What have you done? Do you have any idea how long it takes to build a monster from cheese?" the troll demanded. "Now how am I going to take over and become King of the Trolls? It will take me years to build another monster as strong and obedient as this one."

"*You* want to be King of the Trolls?" Princess Pulverizer asked him.

"Yeah," the troll said. "Why *not* me? Are you saying I can't?"

"Well, I—" Princess Pulverizer began.

"Is it because I have pink hair?" the troll continued. "Just because my brothers and sisters all have purple and green hair doesn't make them better or stronger than I am. I like having pink hair."

"Pink hair is lovely," Princess Pulverizer agreed. "It's not the reason you—"

"When I become king, I'm going to make all the trolls bow to me and do whatever I tell them to do," the troll continued.

"That's mean," Lucas said.

"Yup," the troll agreed proudly. "I'm plenty mean."

"That's the problem," Princess Pulverizer told him. "Good kings aren't mean."

"Who says?" the troll demanded.

"Nobody. It's just the way it is," the princess explained. "A king has to inspire people to *want* to follow his lead. And you . . ."

"And I *what*?" the troll demanded furiously.

"Well, the only follower you have is this guy." Princess Pulverizer pointed to the monster. "And you had to *build* him."

"Out of stinky cheese," the troll pointed out. "I figured if his muscles didn't defeat my enemies, his smell sure would. Pretty smart, huh?"

Not *that* smart. Princess Pulverizer wanted to point out that the troll's cheese monster couldn't even beat two kids and a dragon. He would never have defeated armies of trolls to make his master the king.

But there was no point in rubbing it in.

"My poor little monster!" the troll sobbed. "My boy. Let me at least save your beautiful cheesy head!" He ran straight into the puddle of slimy, runny cheese.

And then the troll stopped. Just like that. He stood there, buried up to his knees in melted cheese.

"I'm stuck!" the troll shouted. "This cheese is hardening around my knees. Somebody get me out of here!"

The only somebodies around were Princess Pulverizer and her friends. And they weren't about to help him.

"I think we should leave," Lucas said.

"Yeah, we already won this battle," Princess Pulverizer agreed. "That troll is going to be stuck there for a long, long time."

"He won't be bothering the people of Ire-Mire-Briar-Shire anymore," Dribble added.

"That's what you think," the troll replied. He looked up. "You forgot, I have another follower. And he's even tougher than my cheese monster."

Squawroark!

"Uh-oh!" Princess Pulverizer gasped. She pointed up to the griffin, who was now flying overhead. "Look who's awake!"

"Now we *really* gotta get out of here!" Lucas started to run. The griffin flew after him.

"Ignore the prisoners!" the troll ordered the griffin. "Just get me out of here."

The griffin did as his master commanded. He turned around in midair and hovered just above the lake of hardening cheese. Then he grabbed the troll by the hair, pulling hard.

"OW!" the troll cried out. "That hurts. And it isn't working. This stuff is like stinky cement. You're going to have to *eat* me out of this mess."

The griffin sniffed at the cheese and shook his head.

"It's not that bad," the troll insisted. "Just start eating."

The griffin had no choice. His master had spoken. He landed at the edge of the lake of hardening cheese, stuck out his birdlike tongue, and ever-so-slowly began to lick at the cheese.

After a few licks, the griffin made a strange face. He grabbed his stomach, and doubled over. And then a big, lion-size blast of gas burst out of his rear end.

"Oh wow," Lucas said. "That stinks."

"I don't think cheese agrees with him," Dribble added.

"Now's our chance," Princess Pulverizer whispered to Dribble and Lucas. "Let's get the cows, sheep, and goats, then scram."

Dribble sniffed at the air. "You don't have to tell me twice," he told her.

"There's just one problem," Lucas pointed out.

"What's that?" Dribble asked him.

"We still don't know how to herd animals," Lucas reminded him. "The only time I ever saw it done, there was a bunch of men on horseback. The horses were the ones leading the cows."

Princess Pulverizer bounced up and down with excitement. "Lucas! You're a genius," she told him. "Herding those animals is going to be easy peasy."

Lucas gave her a funny look. "How? We don't have a horse."

"No," Princess Pulverizer replied. "But we have a *dragon*."

"Me?" Dribble asked. "What do I . . ." He paused. Then he shook his head. "Oh no. No way," he told the princess.

"Come on, Dribble. If a horse can do it, surely a dragon can." The princess scrambled up onto his back.

"I am not a horse. And I am not herding those animals," Dribble insisted. "You're just going to have to find another way."

"She's right, Dribble," Lucas pleaded. "You're our only hope. And I don't think I can stand being in this stinky place one more minute."

Dribble sniffed at the foul-smelling air. "Okay, I'll do it," he agreed finally. "Just this once. But if either of you two ever tell anyone about this, I'll . . . I'll—"

"Don't worry," Princess Pulverizer assured him. "Your secret is safe with us. Now, giddyap! We have some herding to do."

CHAPTER 10

"That's the last of them," Lucas said as he locked a small sheep into a barn near the center of Ire-Mire-Briar-Shire.

"Herding animals sure is hard work," Princess Pulverizer remarked.

Dribble gave her a look. "What did *you* do? I'm the one who was running around getting them to move. You were just sitting on my back."

"I was yelling 'giddyap,'" she reminded him. "My throat is scratchy."

Dribble rolled his eyes.

The farmers of Ire-Mire-Briar-Shire had all gathered around Princess Pulverizer and her friends. The princess turned and greeted them.

"We are glad that we could return all your animals to you," she told them with a big smile.

But the farmers did not smile back. Neither did the shopkeepers, the children, or the mayor. They all had sour looks on their faces.

This was not what the princess had expected at all.

"What's wrong?" Lucas asked.

"It's this stink in the air," the mayor explained.

"That's the smell of spoiled cheese," Dribble told him. "And griffin gas."

"Griffins pass a lot of gas," Princess Pulverizer added. "You can smell it for miles."

"How do you expect us to live like this?" an old woman asked the princess. "Could *you* live like this?"

Princess Pulverizer frowned. No, she could not.

But that wasn't the point. She had done what she had said she would do. Sure, it hadn't turned out perfectly. But she had brought the animals back. She had done her good deed. She was supposed to get praise and cheers, maybe a key to the village, and some roses, and . . .

ROSES!

That was it.

"I can fix this smelly situation," Princess Pulverizer told the mayor. "Easy peasy."

"I hate when she says that," Dribble whispered to Lucas. "It usually means she takes it easy while I do the work."

"All you have to do is plant flowers," Princess Pulverizer told the mayor. "Lots and lots of flowers. And pine trees. Pine smells nice. Then the nice smells will block out the bad ones."

"That's a wonderful idea," the mayor declared.

Princess Pulverizer stood tall. She was quite pleased with herself.

"Except for one thing," the mayor continued.

Princess Pulverizer slumped. She did *not* like the sound of that.

"We don't have a lot of flowers or pine trees in Ire-Mire-Briar-Shire," the mayor explained.

Princess Pulverizer scowled. Honestly, did she have to do *everything* for these people?

"You can buy them from neighboring villages," she told the mayor. "Or transplant some trees from the forest."

"That's a wonderful idea!" the mayor of Ire-Mire-Briar-Shire declared again.

"Except for one other thing."

"And what's that?" Princess Pulverizer asked.

"Who here is strong enough to carry a tree?" the mayor replied.

"Oh, that's easy," Princess Pulverizer said. "Dribble is strong. He can carry trees."

Dribble shook his head. "See what I mean? *She* says easy peasy and *I* do all the work."

Lucas looked at Princess Pulverizer. "You're going to help plant flowers, too, right?" he asked her.

Princess Pulverizer frowned. She hadn't planned on planting. She had planned on being in charge of the *other people* planting.

But now that everyone was staring at her . . .

"Sure," she agreed. "Of course. Knights don't mind getting their hands dirty when they have to."

Dribble gave her a smile. "That's more like it," he told her.

With everyone working together, it didn't take long for Ire-Mire-Briar-Shire to start smelling sweet.

And the flowers brought an extra bonus—honeybees. Hundreds of them were buzzing all around the flowers.

"You're going to have a lot of honey soon," Princess Pulverizer told the mayor.

"I love honey," Dribble said. "I have a great recipe for melted brie and honey on a sesame roll. Maybe I will come back someday and make it for you."

"That would be wonderful!" the mayor said. "In the meantime, the people of Ire-Mire-Briar-Shire have a gift for you three. It's a small token of our gratitude."

The mayor held out a long arrow with orange and yellow feathers. "This is for you," he said as he handed it to Princess Pulverizer.

"Thank you," the princess replied. She was surprised. It didn't seem like much of a token, considering how much she and her friends had done to help the village.

But she didn't say that. Because saying anything other than "thank you" would be rude. And knights were never rude.

"This is not just any arrow," the mayor continued. "It is a *magic* arrow. Someday you might find it quite helpful. If ever the holder of the arrow finds themselves lost, the arrow will always point them toward home."

Princess Pulverizer brightened. That was more like it.

"Ouch!" Suddenly Lucas let out a shout. "That hurt."

"What's the matter, little buddy?" Dribble asked him.

"A bee stung me!" Lucas answered.
"I gotta get out of here. I hate bees!"
He started to run up the road. Then he
stopped and looked at the people of
Ire-Mire-Briar-Shire. "I'm sorry. I forgot
to say goodbye. So, goodbye! *OW!*"
He took off down the road again.

"I guess that's our cue to leave,"
Princess Pulverizer told the mayor.
"Thank you very much for the arrow."

"Thank *you* for all you have done for
our little village," the mayor replied.

"You're welcome," Dribble and Princess
Pulverizer said.

"Help!" Lucas shouted. "Get this bee
away from me."

Princess Pulverizer giggled. "Sounds
like we've got someone else to help,"
she told Dribble—although she doubted

shooing away a bee could be counted toward her Quest of Kindness.

Dribble smiled and nodded. "Wait up, little buddy!" he called to Lucas. "We're on our way!"

As Princess Pulverizer hurried down the road, she could hear the town singing a special song in her honor—

"For *cheese* a jolly good fellow. For *cheese* a jolly good fellow. For *cheese* a jolly good fellow. Which nobody can deny!"

the quest continues . . .

and now, here's a sneak peek at the next

Princess Pulverizer

Quit Buggin' me!

"I wanna play! I wanna play!" Dribble shouted excitedly.

The ground shook beneath the big green dragon as he jumped up and down. He pointed toward the group of kids who had gathered in the middle of the town square. "I bet I can break that piñata with one swing!" he boasted.

"I don't think those kids need any

help," Dribble's best friend, a knight-in-training named Lucas, said. "That last kid got really close to hitting it."

But Dribble didn't hear Lucas. He was already halfway down the road, bouncing toward the square, shouting, *"I wanna play! I wanna play!"*

"I wish he would stop jumping." Princess Pulverizer groaned, tossing her long braid over her shoulder. "All this shaking is giving me a bellyache."

"That could also be from the four grilled cheddar cheese on rye sandwiches you had for breakfast," Lucas pointed out.

Princess Pulverizer shrugged. "Dribble makes delicious grilled cheese. I couldn't help myself." The earth shook beneath her feet. "Whoa!" she exclaimed.

"That *was* a big one," Lucas agreed.

"Come on," Princess Pulverizer urged him. "We better catch up to Dribble before he breaks something. And I don't mean the piñata."

"AAAAAHHHHHHH!"

Princess Pulverizer and Lucas reached the town square in time to see all the children running off to hide—leaving Dribble alone by the piñata.

"I just wanted to play with them," Dribble said sadly, looking around the empty square.

to Be continued . . .

PRINCESS PULVERIZER

COLLECT EACH ADVENTURE ON YOUR READING QUEST!

NANCY KRULIK

is the author of more than two hundred books for children and young adults, including three *New York Times* Best Sellers. She is the creator of several successful book series for children, including Katie Kazoo, Switcheroo; How I Survived Middle School; George Brown, Class Clown; and Magic Bone.

BEN BALISTRERI

has been working for more than twenty years in the animation industry. He's won an Emmy Award for his character designs and has been nominated for nine Annie Awards, winning once. His art can be seen in *Tangled: The Series*, *How to Train Your Dragon*, and many more.